CLOWN AROUND

Written by Dana Meachen Rau
Illustrated by Nate Evans

Reading Advisers:

Gail Saunders-Smith, Ph.D., Reading Specialist

*Dr. Linda D. Labbo, Department of Reading Education,
College of Education, The University of Georgia*

LEVEL B

A COMPASS POINT
EARLY READER

For Larry Dane Brimner

A Note to Parents

As you share this book with your child, you are showing your new reader what reading looks like and sounds like. You can read to your child anywhere—in a special area in your home, at the library, on the bus, or in the car. Your child will associate reading with the pleasure of being with you.

This book will introduce your young reader to many of the basic concepts, skills, and vocabulary necessary for successful reading. Talk through the details in each picture before you read. Then read the book to your child. As you read, point to each word, stopping to talk about what the words mean and the pictures show. Your child will begin to link the sounds of the letters with the look of the words that you and he or she read.

After your child is familiar with the story, let him or her read the story alone. Be careful to let the young reader make mistakes and correct them on his or her own. Be sure to praise the young reader's abilities. And, above all, have fun.

Gail Saunders-Smith, Ph.D.
Reading Specialist

Compass Point Books
151 Good Counsel Drive
P.O. Box 669
Mankato, MN 56002-0669

Visit Compass Point Books on the Internet at *www.compasspointbooks.com* or e-mail your request to *custserv@compasspointbooks.com*

Library of Congress Cataloging-in-Publication Data

Rau, Dana Meachen, 1971–
    Clown around / by Dana Meachen Rau ; illustrated by Nate Evans.
        p. cm. — (Compass Point early reader)
    Summary: A clown troupe prepares for, and presents, a circus act complete with seltzer, a tiny car, and a high wire act.
    ISBN-13: 978-0-7565-0074-0 (library binding)
    ISBN-10: 0-7565-0074-5 (library binding)
    ISBN-13: 978-0-7565-2222-3 (paperback)
        [1. Clowns—Fiction. 2. Circus—Fiction. 3. Stories in rhyme.] I. Evans, Nate, ill.
II. Title. III. Series.
    PZ8.3.R232 Cl 2001
    [E]—dc21   00-011846

Some clowns are ready.

Some clowns are slow.

They all get dressed
for the big show!

Clowns squeeze in.

Clowns burst out!

"Welcome to the circus!"
the clowns shout.

Clowns duck low.

Clowns ride high.

These crazy clowns can even fly!

Clowns can whisper.
Clowns can shout.

Clowns choose friends to help them out.

Clowns stack up.

"Clowns fall down!

It's lots of fun
to clown around.

More Fun with Clowns!

Look at the clown faces to the right together with your child and talk about different feelings. See if your child can match the clown faces with the words below:

friendly

surprised

tired

mad

sad

happy

Ask your child what other feelings he or she can think of to match these clown faces. Urge him or her to draw a clown face showing one or more of the feelings shown here.

Word List

(In this book: 45 words)

all	fall	ride
are	fly	shout
around	for	show
big	friends	slow
burst	fun	some
can	get	squeeze
choose	help	stack
circus	high	the
clown	in	them
clowns	it's	these
crazy	lots	they
down	low	to
dressed	of	up
duck	out	welcome
even	ready	whisper

About the Author

When Dana Meachen Rau was only three, she went to the circus for the first time. She loved watching the clowns. Her biggest wish was to ride crammed inside a tiny clown car. Today, Dana still clowns around every day with her son, Charlie, and husband, Chris. Sometimes she does work, too, in her office at home in Farmington, Connecticut.

About the Illustrator

Nate Evans lives in Los Angeles, California. He worked as an artist at a major greeting card company for nine years before leaving to work as a freelance illustrator. Since then, he has illustrated more than thirty books and written two books of his own. He has also created numerous posters, puzzles, and sticker sheets. The illustrations for this book were done with watercolor paints and colored pencils.